MORE OF THE SAME

MORE OF THE SAME

Some Author

MMXVI
Armchair Adventure
Bodegraven, The Netherlands

More of the Same / Some Author. - Bodegraven : Armchair Adventure, 2016. -
116 p. ; 23 cm. - (Armchair Adventure Publication ; 1).
ISBN 978-90-825194-0-2

Available on lulu.com.
Also available in Dutch, German, French and Spanish.

Contents

Chapter I   7

Chapter II   25

Chapter III   42

Chapter IV   59

Chapter V   76

Chapter VI   95

Chapter VII   111

Chapter I

More of the same. More of the same.

More of the same. More

of the same. More of the same.
More of the same. More of the same.
More of the same. More of the same.

same. More of the same.

More of the same. More of the same.

More of the same. More of the same. More of the same. More of the same. More of the same. More of the same. More of the same. More of the same. More of the same. More of the same. More of the same. More of the same. More of the same. More of the same. More of the same. More of the same. More of the same. More of the same.

More of the same. More of the same.

More of the same. More of

the same. More of the same.

More of the same. More of the same.

More of the same. More of the same.

More of the same. More of the

same. More of the same.

More of the same. More of the same.

More of the same. More of the same. More of the same. More of the same. More of the same. More of the same. More of the same. More of the same. More of the same. More of the same. More of the same. More of the same. More of the same. More of the

same. More of the same.

More of the same. More of the same.

More of the same. More of the same. More of the same. More of the same. More of the same. More of the same. More of the same. More of the same. More of the same. More of the same. More of the same. More of the same.

More of the same. More of the same.

More of the same. More of the

same. More of the same.

More of the same. More of the same.

More of the same. More of the same.

More of the same. More of the same.

More of the same. More of the same.

More of the same. More of the same.

More of the same. More of the same.

More of the same. More of

the same. More of the same.

More of the same. More of the same.

More of the same. More of the same. More of the same. More of the same. More of the same. More of the same. More of the same. More of the same. More of the same. More of the same. More of the same. More of the same. More of the same.

More of the same. More of the same.
More of the same. More of the

same. More of the same.

More of the same. More of the same.

More of the same. More of the same. More of the same. More of the same. More of the same. More of the same. More of the same. More of the same. More of the same. More of the same. More of the same. More of the same. More of the same. More of the same. More of the same. More of the same. More of the same. More of the same.

More of the same. More of the same.

More of the same. More of the same.

More of the same. More of the

same. More of the same.

More of the same. More of the same.

More of the same. More of the same.

More of the same. More of the

same. More of the same.

More of the same. More of the same.

More of the same. More of the same.

More of the same. More of

the same. More of the same. More of the same. More of the same. More of the same. More of the same. More of the same. More of the same. More of the same. More of the same.

More of the same. More of the same.

More of the same. More of the same.

More of the same. More

of the same. More of the same. More of the same. More of the same. More of the same. More of the same. More of the same. More of the same. More of the same. More of the same. More of the same. More of the same. More of the same. More of the same. More of the same. More of the same.

More of the same. More of the same.

More of the same. More of the same.

More of the same. More of the same.

More of the same. More

of the same. More of the same.

More of the same. More of the same.

More of the same. More of the same.

Chapter II

More of the same. More

of the same. More of the same.

More of the same. More of the same.

More of the same. More of the same.

More of the same. More of the same. More of the same. More of the same. More of the same. More of the same. More of the same. More of the same. More of the same. More of the same. More of the same. More of the same. More of the same. More of the same. More of the same. More of the same.

More of the same. More of the same. More of the same. More of the same. More of the same. More of the same. More of the same. More of the same. More of the same. More of the same. More of the same. More of the same. More of the same. More of the same. More of the same. More of the same. More of the same. More of the same. More of the same. More of the same.

More of the same. More of the same.

More of the same. More of the same.

More of the same. More of the same. More of the same. More of the same. More of the same. More of the same. More of the same. More of the same. More of the same. More of the same. More of the same. More of the same. More of the same. More of the same. More of the same.

More of the same. More of the same.

More of the same. More of the same.

More of the same. More of

the same. More of the same. More of the same. More of the same. More of the same. More of the same. More of the same. More of the same. More of the same. More of the same. More of the same.

More of the same. More of the same.

More of the same. More of

the same. More of the same.

More of the same. More of the same.

More of the same. More of the same.

More of the same. More of the same. More of the same. More of the same. More of the same. More of the same. More of the same. More of the same. More of the same. More of the same. More of the same. More of the same. More of the same. More of the same.

More of the same. More of the same. More of the same. More of the same. More of the same. More of the same. More of the same. More of the same. More of the same. More of the same. More of the same. More of the same. More of the same. More of the same. More of the same. More of the same.

More of the same. More of the same. More of the same. More of the same. More of the same. More of the same. More of the same. More of the same. More of the same. More of the same. More of the same. More of the same. More of the same. More of the same. More of the same.
More of the same. More of the same. More of the same. More of the same. More of the same. More of the same. More of the same. More of the same. More of the same. More of the same. More of the same. More of the same. More of the same. More of the same. More of the same. More of the same. More of the same.
More of the same. More of the same. More of the same. More of the same. More of the same. More of the same. More of the same. More of the same. More of the same. More of the same. More of the same. More of the same. More of the same. More of the same. More of the same. More of the same. More of the same.
More of the same. More of the same. More of the same. More of the same. More of the same. More of the same. More of the same. More of the same. More of the same. More of the same. More of the same. More of the same. More of the same. More of the same. More of the same. More of the same. More of the same.
More of the same. More of the same. More of the same. More of the same. More of the same. More of the same. More of the same. More of the same. More of the same. More of the same. More of the same. More of the same. More of the same. More of the same. More of the same. More of the same. More of the same.
More of the same. More of the same. More of the same. More of the same. More of the same. More of the same. More of the same. More of the same. More of the same. More of the same. More of the same. More of the same. More of the same. More of the same. More of the same. More of the same. More of the same.
More of the same. More of the same. More of the same. More of the same. More of the same. More of the same. More of the same. More of the same. More of the same. More of the same. More of the same. More of the same. More of the same. More of the same.
More of the same. More of the

same. More of the same. More of the same. More of the same. More of the same. More of the same. More of the same. More of the same.

More of the same. More of the same.

More of the same. More of the same.

More of the same. More of the same.

More of the same. More of

the same. More of the same. More of the same. More of the same. More of the same. More of the same. More of the same.
More of the same. More of the same.
More of the same. More of the same.
More of the same. More of the same.

More of the same. More of the same.
More of the same.
More of the same. More of the same.
More of the same. More of the same. More of the same. More of the same. More of the same. More of the same. More of the same. More of the same. More of the same. More of the same. More of the same. More of the same. More of the

same. More of the same.

More of the same. More of the same.

More of the same. More of the same.

More of the same. More of the same. More of the same. More of the same. More of the same. More of the same. More of the same. More of the same. More of the same. More of the same. More of the same. More of the same. More of the

same. More of the same. More of the same. More of the same. More of the same. More of the same. More of the same. More of the same.

More of the same. More of the same.

More of the same. More of the same.

More of the same. More of the same. More of the same. More of the same. More of the same. More of the same. More of the same. More of the same.

More of the same. More of the same.

More of the same. More of the same.

More of the same. More of the same.

More of the same. More of the same. More of the same. More of the same. More of the same. More of the same. More of the same. More of the same. More of

the same. More of the same.

More of the same. More of the same.

More of the same. More of the same.

More of the same. More of the same.

More of the same. More of the same.

More of the same. More of the same.

More of the same. More of the

same. More of the same.

More of the same. More of the same.

More of the same. More of

the same. More of the same.

More of the same. More of the same.

Chapter III

More of the same. More of the same.

More of the same. More of the same.

More of the same. More of the same. More of the same. More of the same. More of the same. More of the same. More of the same. More of the same. More of the same. More of the same. More of the same. More of the same. More of the same. More of the same. More of the same. More of the same. More of the same. More of the same. More of the same.

More of the same. More of the same.

More of the same. More of the same. More of the same. More of the same. More of the same. More of the same. More of the same. More of the same. More of the same. More of the same. More of the same. More of the same. More of the samc. Morc of thc samc. Morc of thc samc. Morc of thc samc. Morc of thc samc. More of the same.

More of the same. More of the same.

More of the same. More of the same.

More of the same. More of the same.

More of the same. More of the same. More of the same. More of the same. More of the same. More of the same. More of the same. More of the same. More of the same. More of the same. More of the same. More of the same. More of the

same. More of the same.

More of the same. More of

the same. More of the same. More of the same. More of the same. More of the same. More of the same.

More of the same. More of the same.

More of the same. More of the same.

More of the same. More of

the same. More of the same.

More of the same. More of the same.

More of the same. More of the same.

More of the same. More of the same. More of the same. More of the same. More of the same. More of the same. More of the same. More of the same. More of the same. More of the same. More of the same. More of the same. More of the

same. More of the same.

More of the same. More of the same.

More of the same. More of the same.

More of the same. More of the same. More of the same. More of the same. More of the same. More of the same. More of the same. More of the same. More of

the same. More of the same.

More of the same. More of the same.

More of the same. More of the same.

More of the same. More of

the same. More of the same. More of the same. More of the same. More of the same. More of the same. More of the same. More of the same. More of the same. More of the same. More of the same.

More of the same. More of the same.

More of the same. More of the same.

More of the same. More of the same.

More of the same. More of the same.
More of the same. More

of the same. More of the same.

More of the same. More of the same.

More of the same. More

of the same. More of the same.

More of the same. More of the same.

More of the same. More of the same.

More of the same. More of the same. More of the same. More of the same. More of the same. More of the same. More of the same. More of the same.

More of the same. More of the same.

More of the same. More of the same.

More of the same. More of the

same. More of the same. More of the same. More of the same. More of the same.
More of the same. More of the same. More of the same. More of the same.
More of the same. More of the same. More of the same. More of the same. More
of the same. More of the same. More of the same. More of the same. More of
the same. More of the same. More of the same. More of the same. More of the
same. More of the same. More of the same. More of the same. More of the same.
More of the same. More of the same. More of the same.
More of the same. More of the same. More of the same. More of the same. More
of the same. More of the same. More of the same. More of the same. More of
the same. More of the same. More of the same. More of the same. More of the
same. More of the same. More of the same. More of the same. More of the same.
More of the same. More of the same. More of the same. More of the same. More
of the same. More of the same. More of the same. More of the same. More of
the same. More of the same. More of the same. More of the same. More of the
same. More of the same. More of the same. More of the same. More of the same.
More of the same. More of the same. More of the same. More of the same. More
of the same. More of the same. More of the same. More of the same. More of
the same. More of the same. More of the same. More of the same. More of the
same. More of the same. More of the same. More of the same. More of the same.
More of the same. More of the same. More of the same. More of the same. More
of the same. More of the same. More of the same. More of the same. More of
the same. More of the same. More of the same. More of the same. More of the
same. More of the same. More of the same. More of the same. More of the same.
More of the same. More of the same. More of the same. More of the same. More
of the same. More of the same. More of the same. More of the same. More of
the same. More of the same. More of the same. More of the same. More of the
same. More of the same. More of the same. More of the same. More of the same.
More of the same. More of the same. More of the same. More of the same. More
of the same. More of the same. More of the same. More of the same. More of
the same. More of the same. More of the same. More of the same. More of the
same. More of the same. More of the same. More of the same. More of the same.
More of the same. More of the same. More of the same. More of the same. More
of the same. More of the same. More of the same. More of the same. More of
the same. More of the same. More of the same. More of the same. More of the
same. More of the same. More of the same.
More of the same. More of the same. More of the same. More of the same. More
of the same. More of the same. More of the same. More of the same. More of
the same. More of the same. More of the same. More of the same. More of the
same. More of the same. More of the same. More of the same. More of the same.

More of the same. More of the same.

More of the same. More of the same.

More of the same. More of the same.

More of the same. More of the same. More of the same. More of the same. More of the same. More of the same. More of the same. More of the same. More of the same. More of the same. More of the same. More of the same. More of the same. More of the same. More of the same. More of the same. More of the same. More of the same. More of the same.

More of the same. More of the same.

More of the same. More of the same.

More of the same. More of the same. More of the same. More of the same. More of the same. More of the same. More of the same. More of the same. More of

the same. More of the same.

Chapter IV

More of the same. More of the same. More of the same. More of the same. More of the same. More of the same. More of the same. More of the same. More of the same. More of the same. More of the same. More of the same. More of the same. More of the same. More of the same. More of the same. More of the same. More of the same. More of the same. More of the same.

More of the same. More of

the same. More of the same. More of the same. More of the same. More of the same. More of the same. More of the same. More of the same. More of the same. More of the same. More of the same.

More of the same. More of the same.

More of the same. More of the

same. More of the same. More of the same. More of the same. More of the same. More of the same. More of the same. More of the same.

More of the same. More of the same.

More of the same. More of the same.

More of the same. More of the same.

More of the same. More of the same. More of the same. More of the same. More of the same. More of the same. More of the same. More of the same. More of the same. More of the same. More of the same. More of the same. More of the same. More of the same. More of the same. More of the same. More of the same. More of the same. More

of the same. More of the same.

More of the same. More of the same.

More of the same. More of the same.

More of the same. More of the same. More of the same. More of the same. More of the same. More of the same. More of the same. More of the same. More of the same. More of the same. More of the same. More of the same. More of the same. More of the same. More of the same. More of the same. More of the same. More of the same.

More of the same. More of the same.

More of the same. More of the same.

More of the same. More of the same.

More of the same. More of

the same. More of the same.

More of the same. More of the same.

More of the same. More of the same.

More of the same. More of the same. More of the same. More of the same. More of the same. More of the same. More of the same. More of the same. More of the same. More of the same. More of the same. More of the same.

More of the same. More

of the same. More of the same. More of the same. More of the same. More of the same. More of the same. More of the same. More of the same.

More of the same. More of the same.

More of the same. More of the same.

More of the same. More of the same. More of the same. More of the same. More of the same. More of the same. More of the same. More of the same. More of the same. More of the same. More of the same. More of the same. More of the

same. More of the same.

More of the same. More of the same.

More of the same. More of the same.

More of the same. More of the same.

More of the same. More of the same. More of the same. More of the same. More of the same. More of the same. More of the same. More of the same. More of the same. More of the same. More of the same. More of the same. More of the same. More of the same. More of the same. More of the same. More of the same. More of the same. More of the same.

More of the same. More of the same. More of the same. More of the same. More of the same. More of the same. More of the same.

More of the same. More of the

same. More of the same. More of the same. More of the same. More of the same. More of the same. More of the same. More of the same. More of the same.

More of the same. More of the same.

More of the same. More of the same. More of the same. More of the same. More of the same. More of the same. More of the same. More of the same. More of the same. More of the same. More of the same. More of the same. More of the same.

More of the same. More of the same.
More of the same. More

of the same. More of the same.

More of the same. More of the same.

More of the same. More of the same.

More of the same. More of the same. More of the same. More of the same. More of the same. More of the same. More of the same. More of the same. More of the same. More of the same. More of the same. More of the same. More of the same. More of the same. More of the same. More of the same. More of the same. More of the same.

More of the same. More of the same.

More of the same. More of the same.

More of the same. More of the same. More of the same. More of the same. More of the same. More of the same. More of the same. More of the same. More of the same. More of the same. More of the same. More of the same. More of the same. More of the same. More of the same. More of the same. More of the same. More of the same. More of the same.

More of the same. More of the same.

More of the same. More of the same.

More of the same. More of the same.

More of the same. More of the same.

More of the same. More of the same. More of the same. More of the same. More of the same. More of the same. More of the same. More of the same. More of the same. More of the same. More of the same. More of the same. More of the same. More of the same. More of the same. More of the same. More of the same.

More of the same. More of the same. More of the same. More of the same. More of the same. More of the same. More of the same. More of the same. More of the same. More of the same. More of the same. More of the same. More of the same. More of the same. More of the same. More of the same. More of the same. More of the same.

More of the same. More of the same.

More of the same. More

of the same. More of the same. More of the same. More of the same. More of the same. More of the same. More of the same. More of the same. More of the same. More of the same. More of the same. More of the same. More of the same. More of the same. More of the same. More of the same.

More of the same. More of the same.

More of the same. More of the same.

More of the same. More of the

same. More of the same.

Chapter V

More of the same. More of the same. More of the same. More of the same. More of the same. More of the same. More of the same. More of the same. More of the same. More of the same. More of the same. More of the same. More of the same. More of the same. More of the same. More of the same. More of the same. More of the same.

More of the same. More of the same.

More of the same. More of the same.

More of the same. More of the same.

More of the same. More of the same.

More of the same. More of

the same. More of the same.

More of the same. More of the same.

More of the same. More of the same.

More of the same. More

of the same. More of the same.

More of the same. More

of the same. More of the same. More of the same. More of the same. More of the same. More of the same.

More of the same. More of the same.

More of the same. More of the same.

More of the same. More of the

same. More of the same.

More of the same. More of the same.

More of the same. More of the same. More of the same. More of the same. More of the same. More of the same. More of the same. More of the same.

More of the same. More of the same.

More of the same. More of the same. More of the same. More of the same. More of the same. More of the same. More of the same. More of the same. More of the same. More of the same. More of the same. More of the same. More of the same. More of the same.

More of the same. More of the same.

More of the same. More of the

same. More of the same.

More of the same. Morc of the samc. Morc of thc samc. Morc of the same. More of the same. More of the same. More of the same. More of the same. More of the same. More of the same. More of the same. More of the same. More of the same. More of the same. More of the same. More of the same. More of the same.

More of the same. More of the same.

More of the same. More

of the same. More of the same. More of the same. More of the same. More of the same. More of the same.

More of the same. More of the same.

More of the same. More of the same.

More of the same. More of the same.

More of the same. More of

the same. More of the same.

More of the same. More of the same.

More of the same. More of the

same. More of the same. More of the same. More of the same. More of the same. More of the same. More of the same. More of the same. More of the same. More of the same. More of the same. More of the same. More of the same. More of the same. More of the same. More of the same. More of the same.

More of the same. More of the same.
More of the same. More of the same.

More of the same. More of

the same. More of the same. More of the same. More of the same. More of the same. More of the same.

More of the same. More of the same. More of the same. More of the same. More of the same. More of the same. More of the same. More of the same. More of the same. More of the same. More of the same. More of the same. More of the same. More of the same. More of the same. More of the same. More of the same. More of the same. More of the same. More of the same.

More of the same. More of the same.

More of the same. More of

the same. More of the same.

More of the same. More of the same.

More of the same. More of the same.

More of the same. More of the same. More of the same. More of the same. More of the same. More of the same. More of the same. More of the same. More of the same. More of the same. More of the same. More of the same. More of the

same. More of the same.

More of the same. More of the same.

More of the same. More of the same.

More of the same. More of the

same. More of the same.

More of the same. More of the same.

More of the same. More of the same.

More of the same. More of the same. More of the same. More of the same. More of the same. More of the same. More of the same. More of the same. More of

the same. More of the same.

More of the same. More of the same.

More of the same. More of the same.

More of the same. More of

the same. More of the same. More of the same. More of the same. More of the same. More of the same. More of the same. More of the same. More of the same. More of the same. More of the same. More of the same. More of the same. More of the same.

More of the same. More of the same.

More of the same. More of

the same. More of the same. More of the same. More of the same. More of the same. More of the same. More of the same. More of the same. More of the same. More of the same. More of the same.

More of the same. More of the same.

More of the same. More of the same.

More of the same. More of the same.

More of the same. More of the same. More of the same. More of the same. More of the same. More of the same. More of the same. More of the same. More of the same. More of the same. More of the same. More of the same. More of the same. More of the same. More of the same. More of the same. More of the same. More of the same.

More of the same. More of the same.

Chapter VI

More of the same. More

of the same. More of the same.

More of the same. More of the same.

More of the same. More of the same.

More of the same. More of the same. More of the same. More of the same. More of the same. More of the same. More of the same. More of the same. More of the same. More of the same. More of the same. More of the same. More of the same. More of the same. More of the same. More of the same. More of the same. More of the same. More of the same.

More of the same. More of the same.

More of the same. More of the same.

More of the same. More

of the same. More of the same.

More of the same. More of the same.

More of the same. More of the same.

More of the same. More of the same.

More of the same. More of the same. More of the same. More of the same. More of the same. More of the same.

More of the same. More of the same. More of the same. More of the same. More of the same. More of the same. More of the same. More of the same. More of the same. More of the same. More of the same. More of the same.

More of the same. More of the same.

More of the same. More of the same.

More of the same. More of the same. More of the same. More of the same. More of the same. More of the same. More of the same. More of the same. More of

the same. More of the same.

More of the same. More of the same.

More of the same. More of the same.

More of the same. More of

the same. More of the same. More of the same. More of the same. More of the same. More of the same. More of the same. More of the same. More of the same. More of the same. More of the same.

More of the same. More of the same.

More of the same. More of the same.

More of the same. More

of the same. More of the same. More of the same. More of the same. More of the same. More of the same.

More of the same. More of the same.

More of the same. More of the

same. More of the same.

More of the same. More of the same.

More of the same. More of the same.

More of the same. More of

the same. More of the same. More of the same. More of the same. More of the same. More of the same. More of the same.

More of the same. More of the same.

More of the same. More

of the same. More of the same.
More of the same. More of the same.
More of the same.
More of the same. More of the same.
More of the same. More of the same. More of the same.
More of the same. More of the same. More of the same. More of the same. More of the same. More of the same. More of the same. More of the same. More of the same. More of the same. More of the same. More of the same. More of the

same. More of the same.

More of the same. More of the same.

More of the same. More of the same.

More of the same. More of the same.

More of the same. More

of the same. More of the same. More of the same. More of the same. More of the same. More of the same. More of the same. More of the same. More of the same. More of the same. More of the same.

More of the same. More of the same.

More of the same. More of the same.

More of the same. More of the same.

More of the same. More of the same. More of the same. More of the same. More of the same. More of the same. More of the same. More of the same. More of the same. More of the same. More of the same. More of the same. More of the

same. More of the same.

More of the same. More of the same. More of the same. More of the same. More of the same. More of the same. More of the same. More of the same. More of the same. More of the same. More of the same. More of the same. More of the same. More of the same. More of the same. More of the same.

More of the same. More of the same.

More of the same. More of the same.

More of the same. More of

the same. More of the same.

More of the same. More of the same. More of the same. More of the same. More of the same. More of the same. More of the same. More of the same. More of the same. More of the same. More of the same. More of the same. More of the same. More of the same. More of the same. More of the same. More of the same. More of the same. More of the same. More of the same.

Chapter VII

More of the same. More of the

same. More of the same.
More of the same.
More of the same. More

of the same. More of the same.
More of the same. More

of the same. More of the same.

More of the same. More of the same.

More of the same. More of the same.
More of the same.

More of the same. More of the same.

More of the same. More of the

same. More of the same.

More of the same. More of the same.

www.ingramcontent.com/pod-product-compliance
Lightning Source LLC
Chambersburg PA
CBHW031843170626
46807CB00004B/1595